Eye To The World
Publishing

HOW DID YOU CREATE ME

Written by Jocelyn Anna Lernout
Illustrated by Zonia Iqbal

Instagram @JocelynAnnaLernout
TikTok @WorldofMajesty

Dedicated to All Children in the World,

May You Live in Joy as a Sparkling Light
with a Glowing Heart Shining Bright!
May All Your Wishes Be Dreams come True.
This is what I Wish for You.

One day while sitting with a tree,
I began to wonder how the world came to be.
So, I opened my heart,
and asked,

"Dear God, Source of All Life,

How did you make me?

Why did you create me?

I would love to know
so I can say thankyou".

"I have eyes to see and ears to hear,
but as I sit here,
I would love to know...

Why do I grow?"

The same day, I was with my mother
and I began to consider
the beauty of life with awe & wonder.
So I asked,

"Dear Mother,
How did you make me?
Why did you create me?
I'd love to know so I can say thankyou.

Why do you teach me
and so kindly guide me
while I learn to see?"

"Let me kiss you and hug you,
so I can thank you".

The same day, I was with my father
and I slowed down to ponder
the joy of life in awe & wonder...
so I asked,
"Dear Father,
How did you make me?
Why did you create me?
I'd love to know."
"Why do you teach me
to be the best I can be?

Let me kiss you and hug you,
so I can thank you."

The next time I was out in nature
I REALLLY saw so many wonderful things
in Creation...
so I sang in Celebration!

"Dear Mother~Father, God, Creator!...
Creation Of All Life!
I see the skies and the trees
I feel the air and fresh breeze.
It is all so amazing to me!"

"Yet, as I wake up
and walk around,
touching my feet to the ground,
I wonder, what does this all mean?!

"Who am I and why am I here?
Who am I here to be?!"

"Dear Mother~Father, Creator, Creation...
How do I find you,
to meet you and greet you,
so I can share thanks?"

God, the Creator of All Life
was grateful to feel the heart
of such a passionate soul.

As gentle whispers of the wind
flew through the sky, Creator responded
to the sweet soul of the child.

"Oh, how beautiful you are...
thankyou for asking with a listening ear.
I'm everywhere, within in your heart,
and among the stars!
Just as green grasses grow wild & free,
I am always here to say hello
among this World of Nature's Majesty!"

The curious soul sat in stillness,
listening to the waves of water
as it whisped by in whispers...
"Whenever you wish to connect about anything,
anytime, anywhere,
I am always here to share.

Remember, the Power of your Heart is strong.
Learn to LISTEN to the Earth,
where you can FEEL how much I care.

Learn to SEE,
there is Beauty & Magic among you, everywhere."

"Wonderful," I said.
"Then I wonder about
a few more things
that may help bring me Peace."

"Why did you make
the skies and the trees...
the storms and the seas?
Can you help me understand please?"

(At times I have felt sad and afraid,
it brought me to my knees...
and yet, I don't choose dis-ease,
I Choose Peace,
Please.)

"Why do I have so many thoughts
and so many dreams!?
Why am I here,
and who am I here to be!?"

On this beautiful day,
Creator was very pleased.
As raindrops of happy tears
came upon the Earth
the Spirit of God revealed Itself.

As a Rainbow of Love lit the sky, a Peaceful
Voice was shared from God's Great Eye,
"O sweet sparkling soul!
You are Divine, here to rise and shine!
There is nothing to fear.
No dream too big, no worry too strong.
All life is a Gift to help guide you along
'The Journey of Your Greatest, Soul Purpose'.
AND you never have to do it alone.
You have Me, within your Heart,
to help Guide you Home."

In this moment
the Sweet Soul
soared high in the sky!
Flying Free with the Magic of
Life!...singing,
"I am Infinitely Alive!
I am here to rise & shine!"

It felt the Magic of Earth
as a living dream;
a special place to learn how to be,
the best version of Soul it could possibly be.

~

It REALLLY loved the feeling
of Flying so Free.

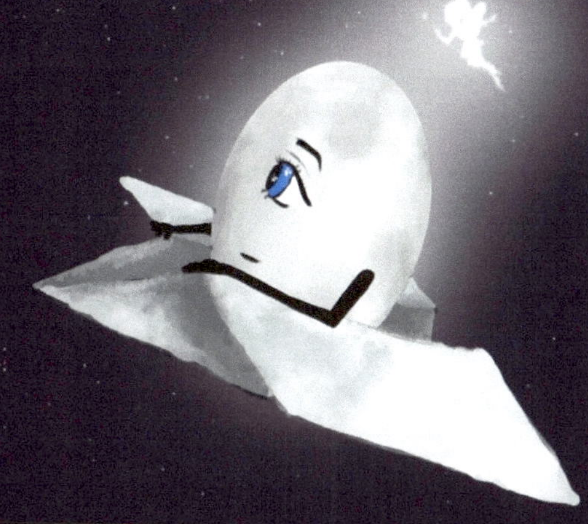

So the Soul slowed down
to enjoy its most Joyous Journey,
Listening to the
whispers of the wind...
"Trust that as you Breathe,
I Breathe with you
and you can surely Know;
All Wishes of your Loving Heart
will be Dreams Come True."

On this special day,
I was on a journey to Remember;
our connection with nature, makes us stronger
so I closed my eyes and listened
to the sweet sounds of inspiration
coming at me
from all
directions.

I realized.... the Voice of my Heart
guides me to the place of my dreams;
the path of my Greatest, Soul Purpose.

Then, with a Glowing Heart,
as the DEEPEST Love I had ever felt,
I shared with the Great Goodness of God,
"Thankyou for all I get to be and see.
Thank Goodness you created me.
I love to share thanks".

Made with A Glowing, Loving Heart
Love & Light All Ways,
JAL

www.ingramcontent.com/pod-product-compliance
Lightning Source LLC
Chambersburg PA
CBHW042132030726
47599CB00002B/450